Elmo's Special Delivery

ACHOO!

By Sarah Albee

Adapted by Eric Furman from "Elmo Says Ach...

Illustrated by Tom Brannon

publications international, ltd.

Play-a-Story™ Animated Storybook

Today Elmo's visiting his grandma and grandpa. Elmo's so happy that *you're* visiting, too. Someone's ringing the doorbell! Elmo loves that sound.

Ding-dong, ding-dong! But who could it be? Wow, it's the mailman with a package! Aw, thank you, Mr. Mailman. Bye-bye. Have a nice day!

SCAN HERE

to:
OSCAR
the Grouch

Is the package for Grandma? No. The post office must have made a mistake!

The package is supposed to go to Oscar the Grouch. Elmo can fix it. Elmo will

take the package to Oscar, just a few blocks away on Sesame Street.

That's funny. Elmo's nose is starting to tickle. But there are no feathers or dandelions near Elmo's nose. Why is Elmo's nose so tickly? Elmo wiggles and twitches and sniffles, but nothing will stop the tickle.

Uh-oh, now Elmo can't help himself.

Excuse Elmo, please.

Maybe something outside is making Elmo sneeze. Elmo will take a shortcut through the grocery store.

Hey, there's Elmo's friend, Bert. Hi, Bert!

Bert is stacking cans, neat and tall, one by one.

One can. AH... Two cans. AH...AH... Three cans.

Whatever's making Elmo sneeze *outside* is making Elmo sneeze *inside*, too.

Boy, this sneezing is slowing Elmo down. Elmo better hurry past this busy barbershop. How much fun would Elmo have getting his hair cut? *Snip, snip, snip!* Uh-oh. Elmo had better grab his hanky.

Elmo sneezes again!

Sesame Street is not far away now. Elmo can't wait to get to Oscar's can to see what's inside this package.

But first Elmo has to pass this long brick wall. It looks brand-new. The bricklayers ask Elmo to look at all the neat bricks. Elmo can see they're very proud of their work.

The wall *is* very nice and strong. But now Elmo feels another tickle.

AH...

AH..

ACHOO!

Okay, that's it! Elmo really wants to know, what is SO SNEEZY around here?

Hey, what's that sound? Not *ah-ah-achoos*, but *a-root-a-toot-toots*.

Oh, look, look, look—here comes a parade!

Elmo wants to watch the elephants march and the super-tall monsters juggle and the colorful clowns make a pyramid.

But Elmo can't forget that he has to deliver Oscar's package and—

Whoa! That's Elmo's BIGGEST sneeze of all!

Okay, this is TOO MUCH sneezing! It is time to deliver this package to Oscar the Grouch. Let's see if Oscar's home.

Knock-knock. Elmo likes that sound, too.

KNOCK-KNOCK-KNOCK, KNOCK-KNOCK, A-KNOCK-KNOCK, KNOCK-KNOCK-KNOCK!

8

Yoo-hoo, Oscar! Elmo knows you're in there. Elmo has a package for you.

Don't you want to see what's inside, Oscar? Elmo does!

Elmo knew Oscar would want his package. Here he is!

Elmo hopes you like your surprise, Oscar. But Elmo can't wait anymore. Elmo wants to know **RIGHT THIS MINUTE** what it is. So does Bert. And the barber. And the bricklayers. And the clowns. (So does Elmo's friend who's reading this book.)

What's inside? Come on, Oscar! Open it!

Oscar tears the paper off the package lickety-split.

Ew! A STINKWEED plant!

EWWWWWWW!

Elmo can't believe his eyes.  Or Elmo's nose.

That stinkweed plant really STINKS!

Oscar says it's the best stinkweed plant he's ever sniffed.

Well, now Elmo knows: even grouches like surprises!

Elmo's glad. Now Elmo's hanky can have a rest from all that sneezing.

Oscar takes a big sniff.

Elmo thinks it might be a good idea for Oscar to have a tissue, too. Here's one. Oscar will need it.

Oscar sniffs one more big sniff. Then he itches. And he twitches. UH-OH. Elmo thinks YOU can guess what happens next!

12